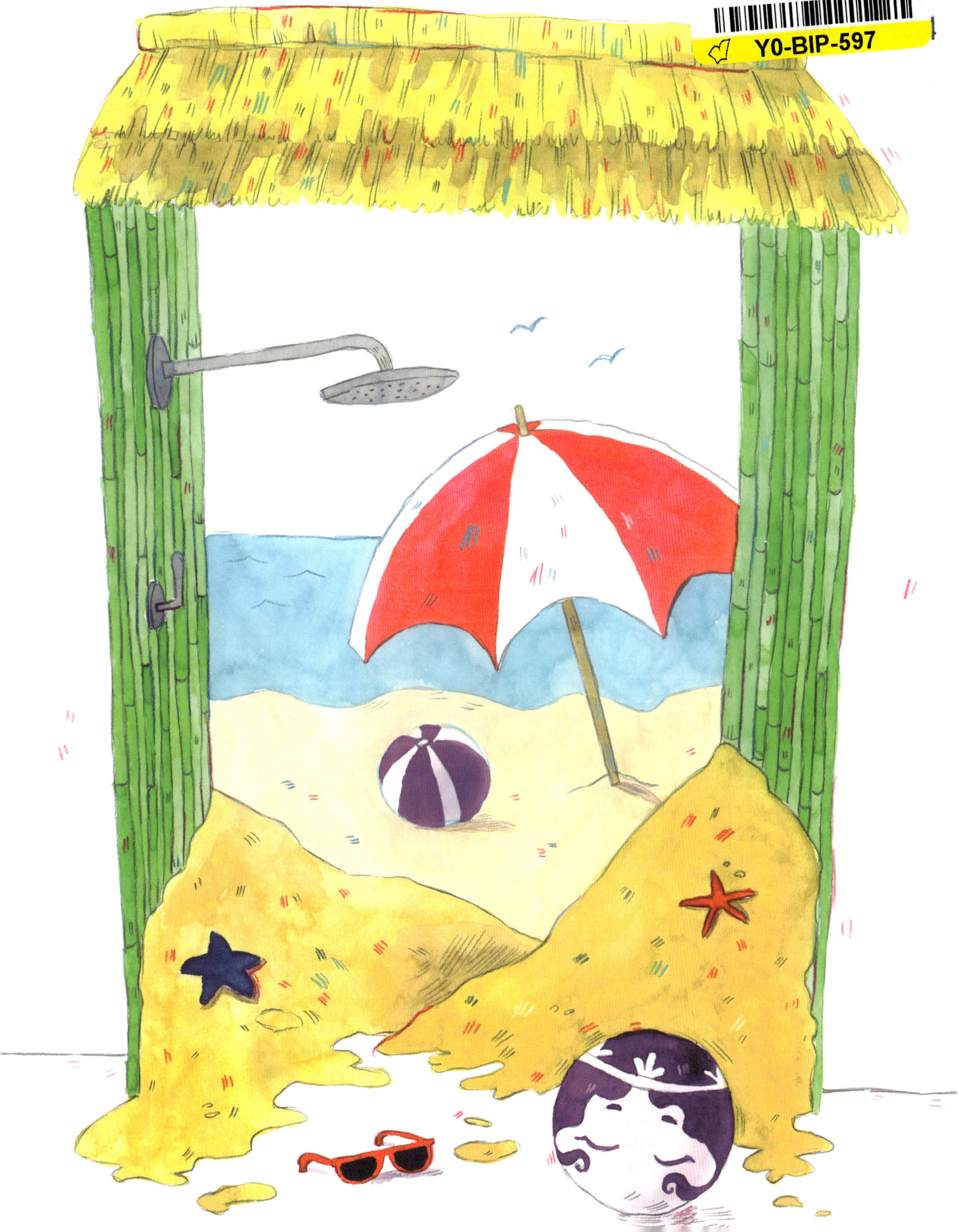

To all the magic spaces that accommodate
our private moments.
—Y.D.

To my bathroom, where I sing in the shower, dream of
new things to paint, and keep all of
my favourite houseplants.
—E.V.

Text copyright © 2023 by Yan Du
Illustrations copyright © 2023 by Erin Vanessa
All rights reserved. No part of this publication may be reproduced, distributed, or transmitted in any form or by any means, electronic, mechanical, photocopying, recording, or otherwise, without the written permission of the publisher, except in the case of brief quotations embodied in critical reviews and certain other noncommercial uses permitted by copyright law. Thank you for your support of the author's rights. If you would like to use material from the book (other than for review purposes), prior written permission must be obtained by contacting the publisher at
permissions@yeehoopress.com.

Published by Yeehoo Press
6540 Lusk Blvd, Ste C152, San Diego, CA 92121
yeehoopress.com

The illustrations for this book were created in watercolor
gouache and pencil crayon.
The book was edited by Peng Shen.
This book was designed by Chao Zhang.
Supervised by Luyang Xue

Library of Congress Control Number: 2022913732
ISBN: 978-1-953458-54-4
Printed in China First Edition
1 2 3 4 5 6 7 8 9 10

My Pocket Bathroom

Written by Yan Du
Illustrated by Erin Vanessa

YEEHOO PRESS

I am a small girl living in a big, big city.
There are voices everywhere . . .

. . . even in my own apartment.

whin

And my room?
Well, I don't really have my own.

and...

Booooooom!

But the bathroom is my sanctuary.

It's small and quiet. And, best of all, I can have
it all to myself as long as I am using it.
It's the safest place . . .

for rehearsing my play,

conducting a concert,

dancing in the steam,

and building bubble castles!

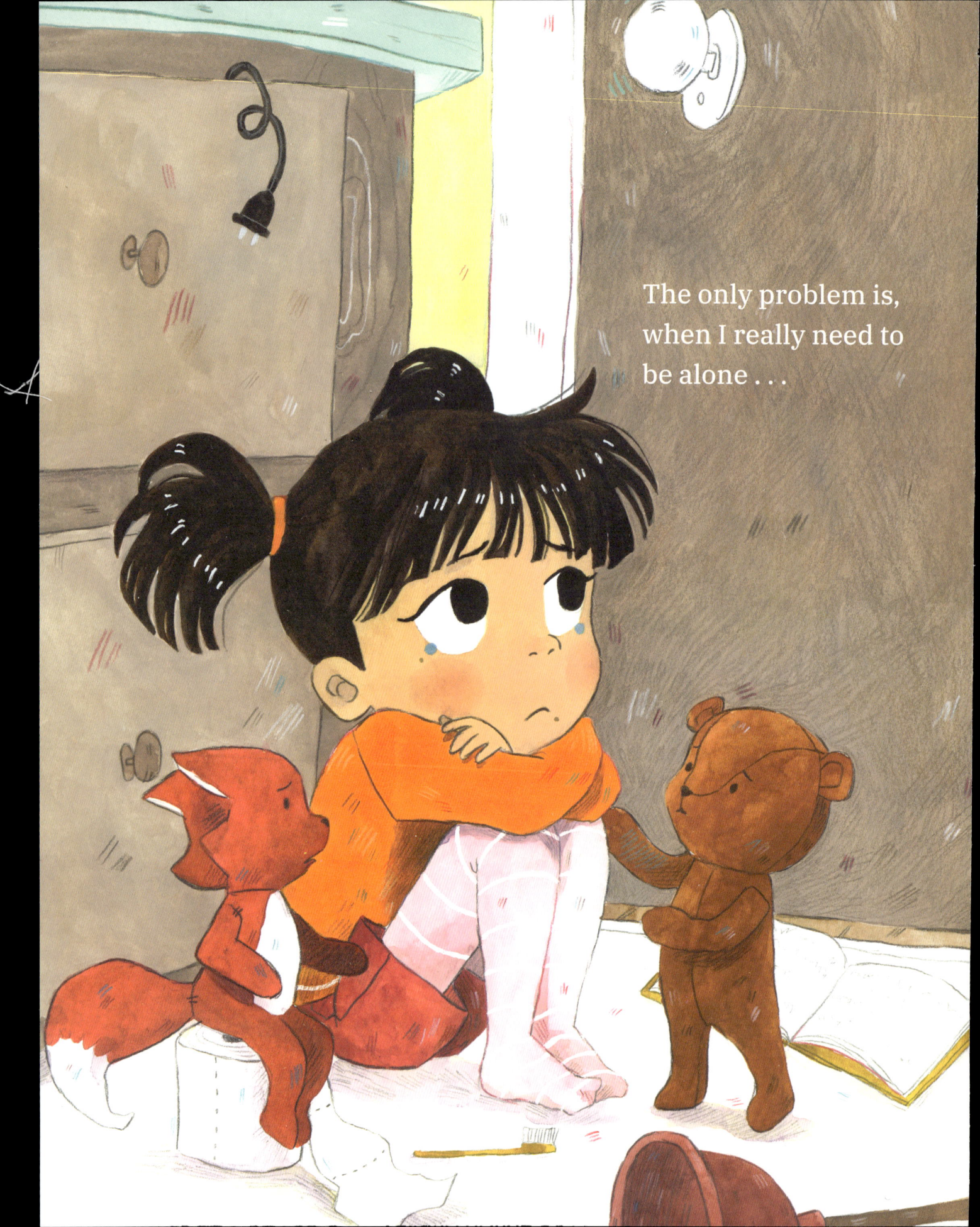

The only problem is, when I really need to be alone . . .

Po, what's taking you so long?

Po, stop wasting water!

Po, what are you doing?

Sometimes I wish I could have the bathroom all to myself.

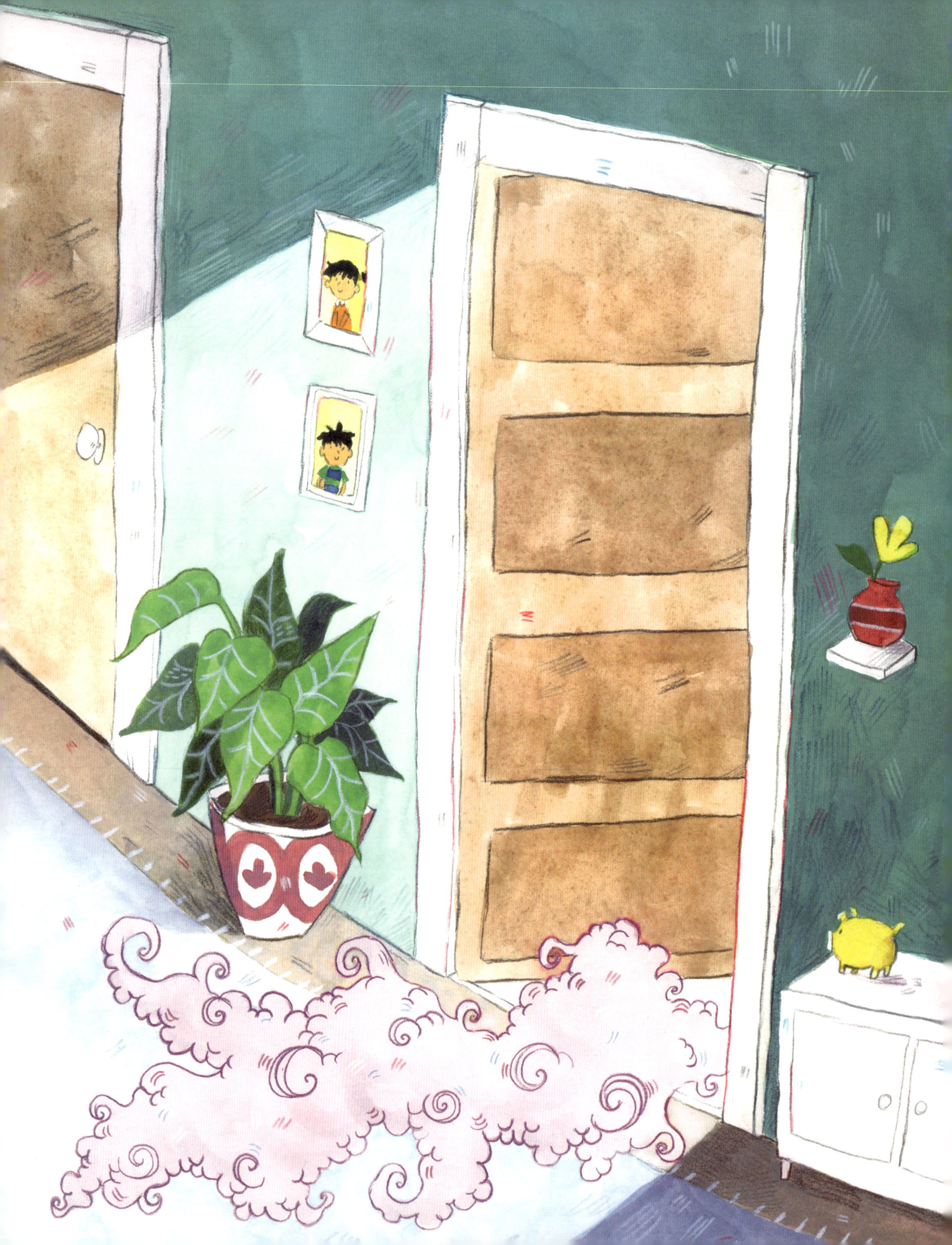

One night, I hear a string of soft laughter coming from the bathroom. Who's there? Curious, I turn around and find . . .

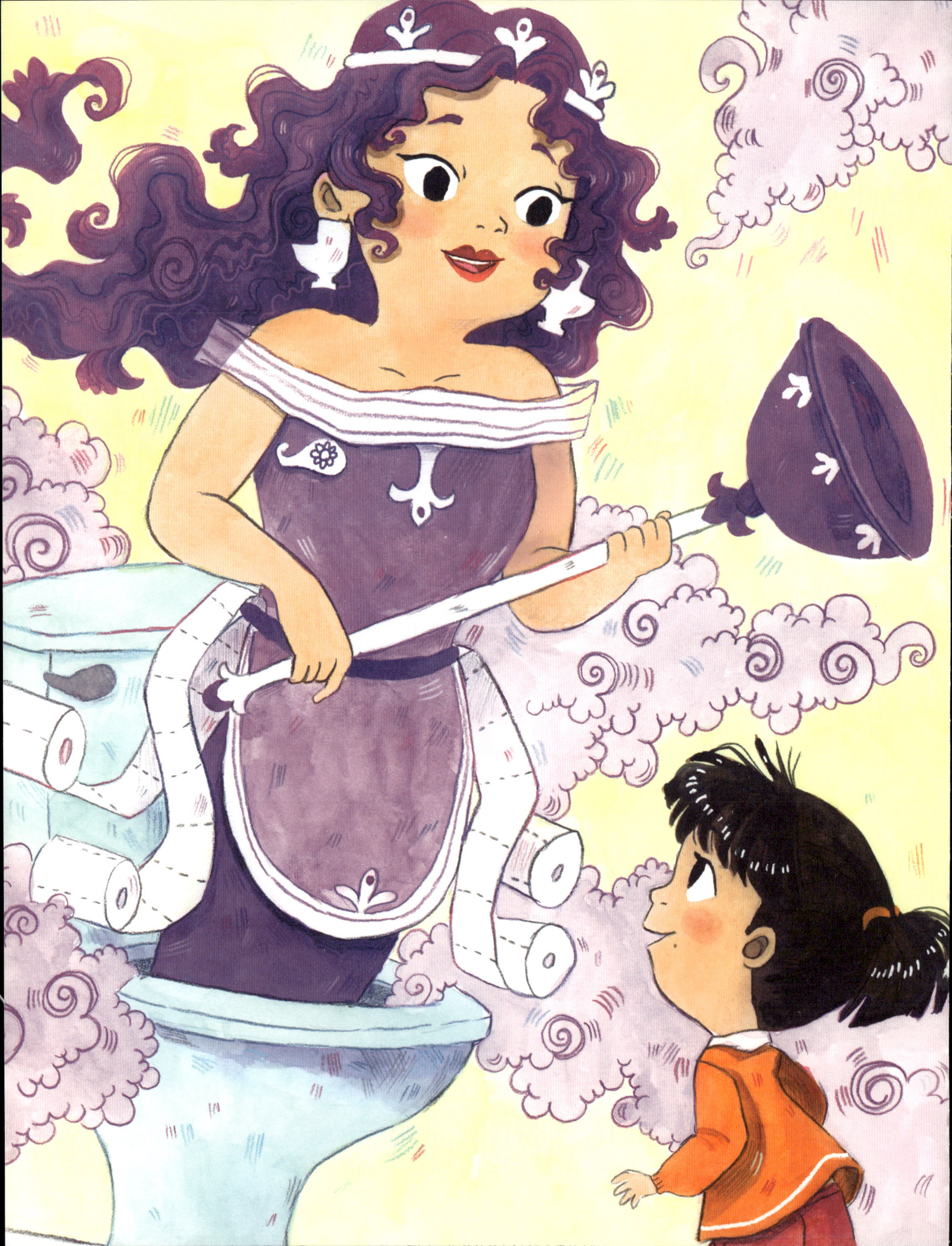

a beautiful lady in a purple dress!

She tells me that she is Lady Violet,
my toilet guardian!

"I have visited many bathrooms in my long life," she says. "But you are the only person who loves your bathroom so much!"

"But . . . it's not really MY bathroom," I sigh.

"I know just what to do," Lady Violet assures me. "Just remember to chant my name whenever you need help."

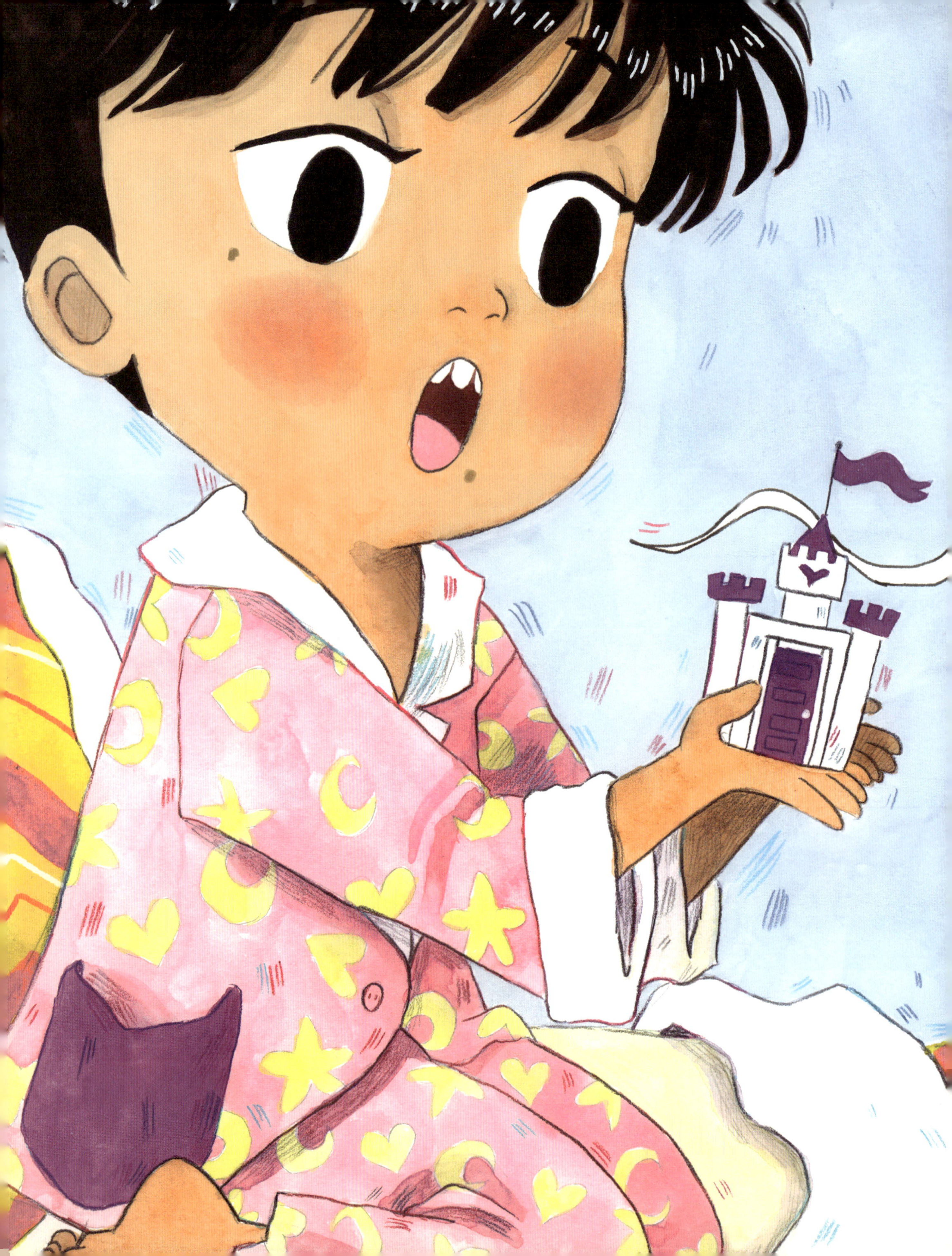

When I wake up the next morning, I notice something bulging inside my pajama pocket.

I reach deep down and guess what I find? The bathroom!

But it's so tiny, I can't even fit my little finger through the door! Then I remember Lady Violet's advice.

Lady Violet, kind and sweet. Lady Violet, help me please!

The tiny bathroom disappears, and a door pops up in the air.

Amazing!

This is my dream bathroom!

From then on, I always take my pocket bathroom with me.

It's a perfect hideout!

I get to slip into my private space whenever I want, wherever I am!

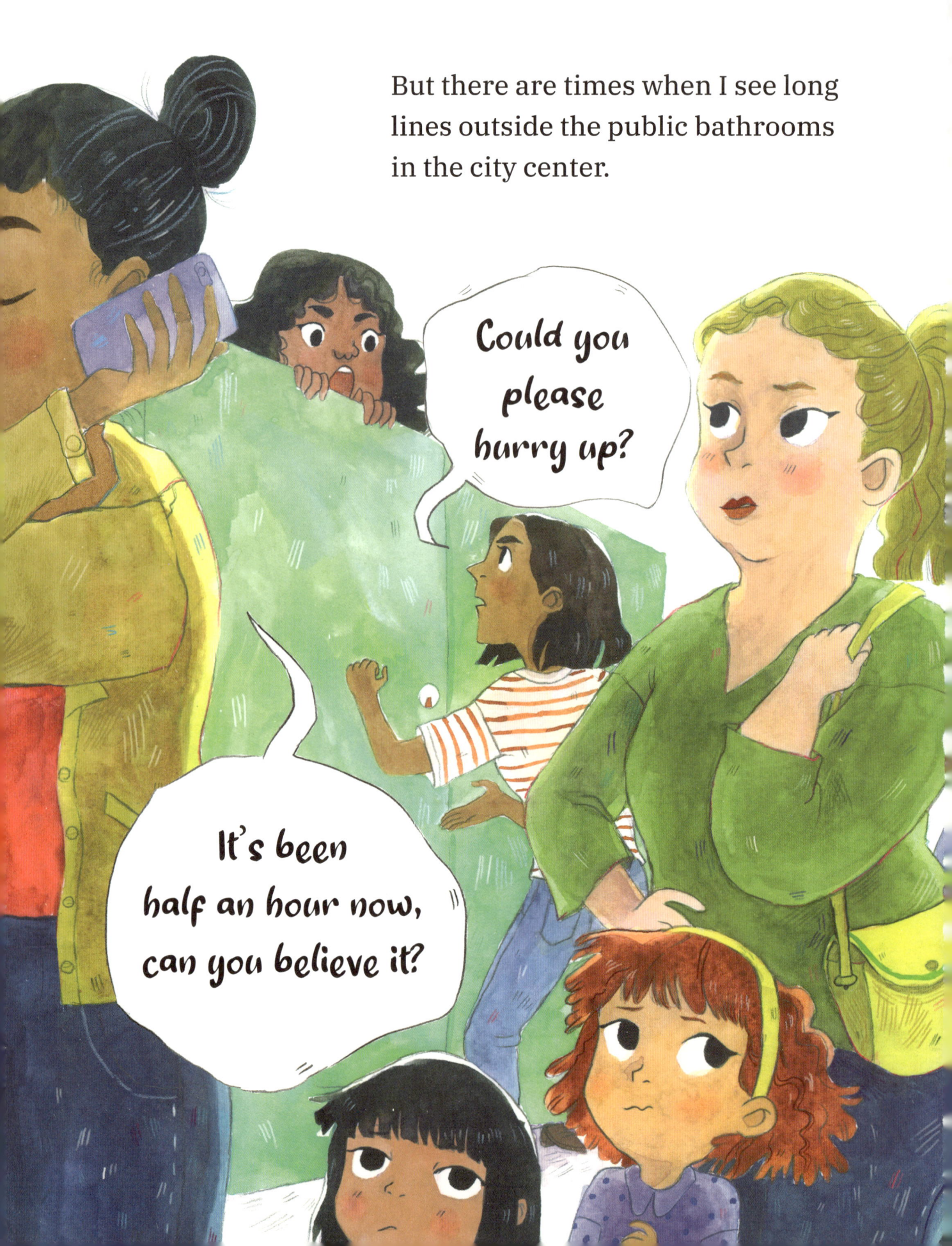

But there are times when I see long lines outside the public bathrooms in the city center.

"Could you please hurry up?"

"It's been half an hour now, can you believe it?"

An idea occurs to me: What if everyone had their own pocket bathroom, like I do? But how?

Hey! You stepped on my foot!

When is it my turn?

Can't ... hold ... on ... much ... longer ...

The next morning, I discover a purple shovel in my schoolbag.
When I see the shovel, I know just what Lady Violet wants me to do.

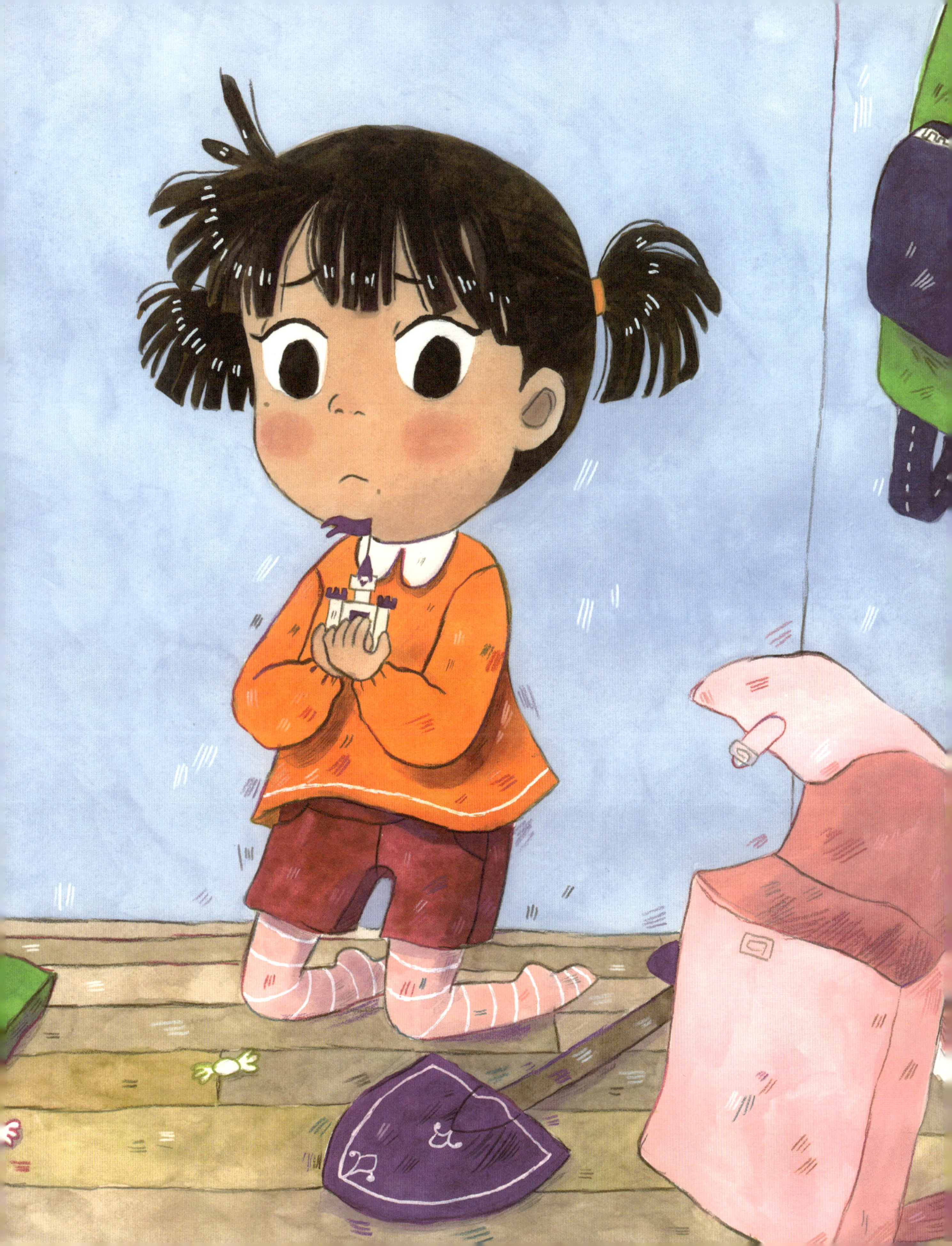

I go to the city park and dig a small hole in the richest soil.

Then I plant my tiny bathroom in the lawn.

When I'm all done,
I chant Lady Violet's name
and wait for the miracle to happen.

Lady Violet, kind and sweet. Lady Violet, help me please!

And it does!
The following day, I pass by the park on my way home and see . . .
a real, prospering BATHROOM TREE for everyone in the city!

Look!

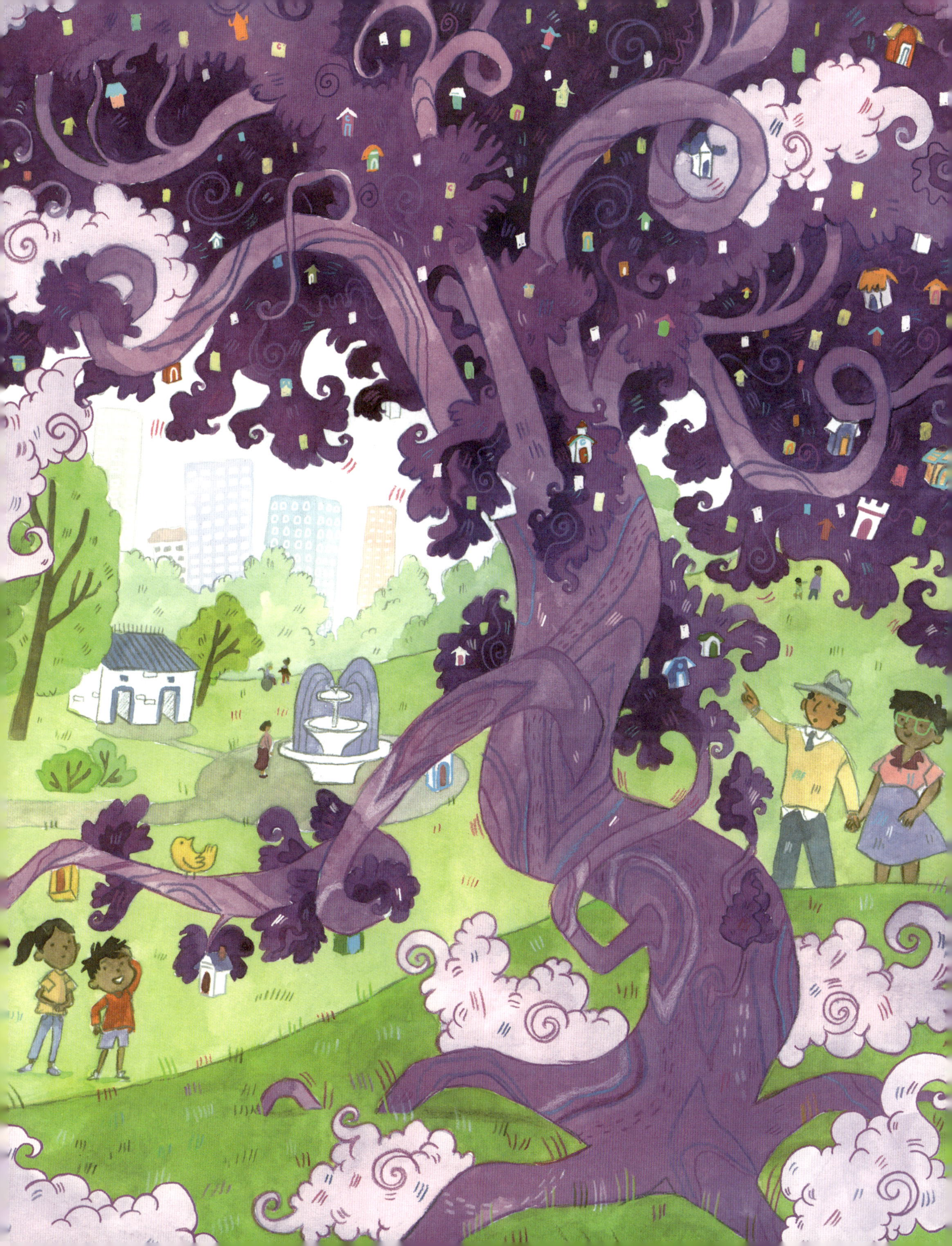

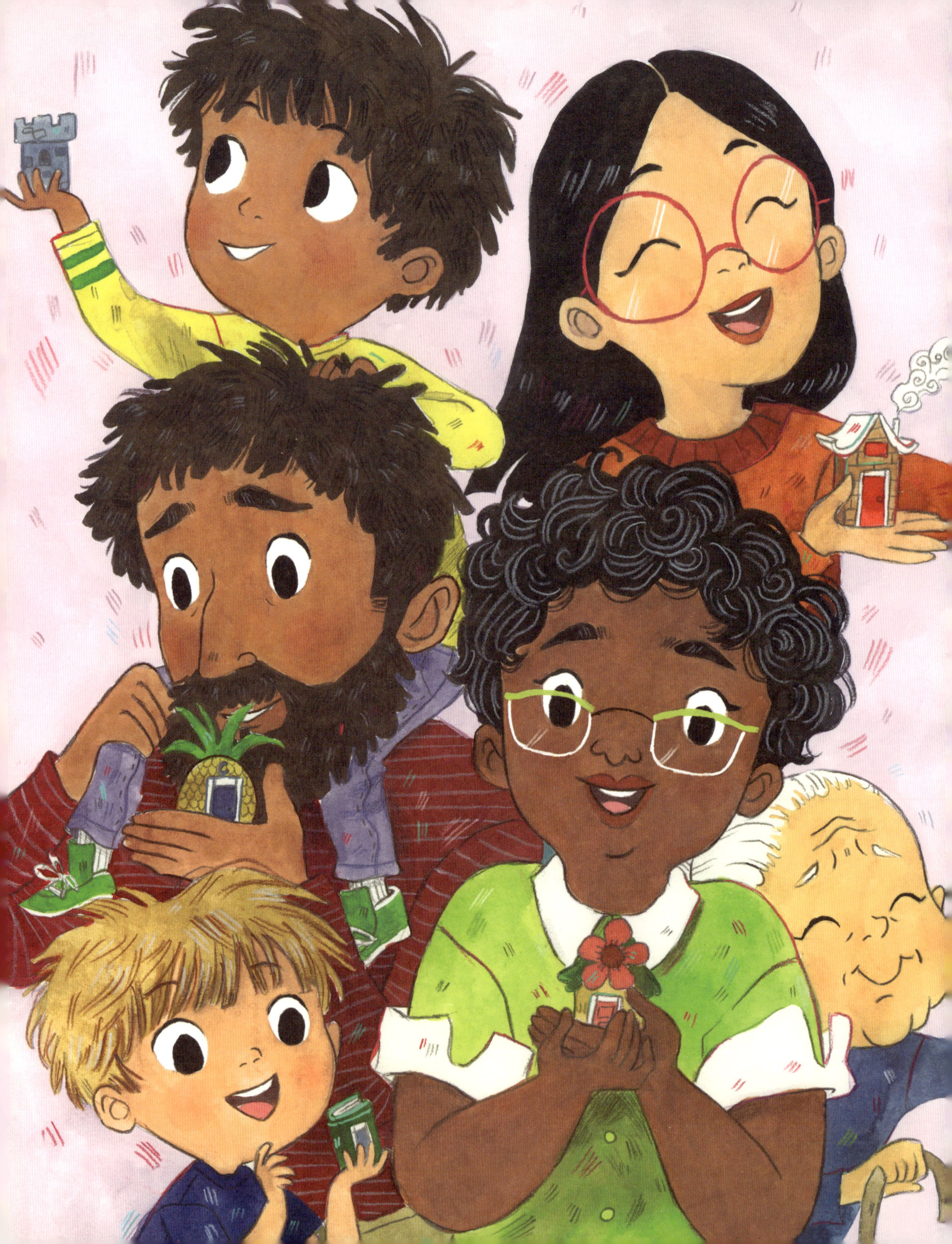

People gather around the tree and pick tiny bathrooms with their names on them.
Everyone's bathroom is different.
There are flower bathrooms, pineapple bathrooms, library bathrooms, beach bathrooms, sauna bathrooms, and bathrooms of every shape and color!

I spot mine immediately.

It hasn't changed a bit since I last used it!

When night falls, I return to my pocket bathroom.
It's the best time of day.
I hope other people are enjoying their time too.

I've always wanted to thank Lady Violet for her help, but I wonder...

Where can she be?

Bathroom gods around the world.

Bathroom gods are timeless creations of the imagination and can be found across a variety of cultural mythologies. More than just guardians of the bathroom, they play a key role in our health and fertility as well.

China

A famous bathroom goddess in Chinese culture is Zigu. There are many versions of her story, and popular legend has it that Zigu lived a sad life and died in the bathroom. Her spirit continued to haunt the bathroom after her death. The gods in heaven, sympathetic to Zigu's misfortunes, made her "the bathroom goddess." Every year, on the night of the 15th of the first month in the Chinese lunar calendar (the day of Zigu's death), women and children make little dolls in her shape and likeness and wait beside the bathroom for her arrival. Zigu also grants peace and fortune to the household and possesses mysterious prophetic skills.

Rome

Cloacina, otherwise known as "the Venus of the Sewers," is the goddess of Rome's oldest drainage system. Her name comes from the Latin word "cloaca" (or drain, sewer). She is the cleanser of the Cloaca Maxima, which channels rainwater into drains to prevent floods. There's also Stercutius, the god of odor, best known for promoting the use of manure in the farming process. And don't forget Crepitus, the god of flatulence. People used to pray to him when they were having stomach troubles.

Japan

Bathroom gods are also popular in Japan. There is a Japanese song that goes, "A beautiful goddess lives in the toilet. If you clean it every day, this goddess will make you into a beautiful woman." Bathroom goddesses are also strongly associated with fertility—it was widely believed that women who made their bathrooms sparkly clean would bear beautiful children.

Many wonderful stories have been told about bathroom gods and goddess all around the world. What other stories do you know about them?

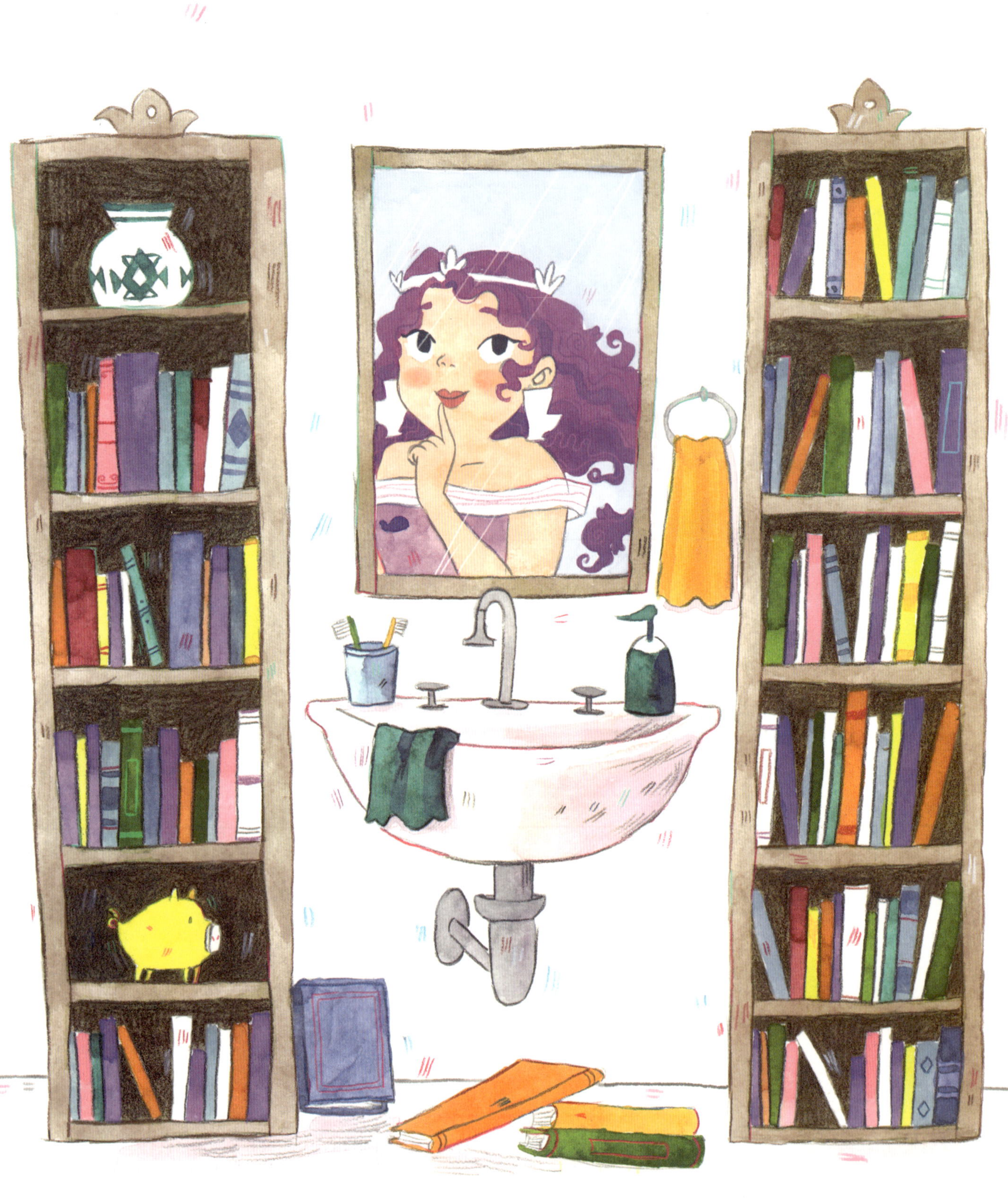